D0535951

Mouldylocks

N
E
W
S

Houghton Mifflin Company Boston 1998

Mouldylocks the witch woke up
one fine sunny morning.
It was her birthday but she wasn't happy.
"No one ever remembers my birthday,"
she said to Hannibal, her cat.
"Cheer up," said Hannibal.
"Here comes the postman, and he's carrying
a long box tied up with ribbon."

Inside the box was a new
magic broomstick.

"Oh, great!" said Mouldylocks.
"My old one is worn out."
But there was no card inside,
so who was it from?

"Well, come on, Hannibal," she said.
"Let's try it out. I hope it goes fast."
And it did - much *too* fast!
It swooped and swished and
looped the loop.

"HELP!" cried Mouldylocks.
"I can't drive this thing."

Suddenly, the broomstick
tipped Mouldylocks and her cat
down a deep dark chimney.
"What's happening?" groaned Mouldylocks.
Then she heard a big shout.

"Happy birthday, Mouldylocks!"
A light came on and there were her three best friends:
the two witches, Crabby Ann and Mama Kano,
and old Wizard Twittle.
They had landed in Wizard Twittle's house.
It was a SURPRISE BIRTHDAY PARTY!

They all gave her birthday gifts.

Crabby Ann gave her a bat-in-a-box.

Mama Kano gave her a pair of talking, walking boots

and Wizard Twittle gave her a pop-up book of spells.

"What party games shall we play?" asked Mouldylocks.
"It's your birthday," said Wizard Twittle. "You choose."
"My favorite game is Pass the Gargoyle,"
said Mouldylocks.

So that's what they played - except for Crabby Ann.
"I hate Pass the Gargoyle," she said. "I always lose."
And she went off in a huff.
"But I bet I'll win at Musical Chairs,"
she muttered to herself.

Crabby Ann did win at Musical Chairs because she bewitched all the chairs. None of them would stay put, except the one on which Crabby Ann was sitting.

Wizard Twittle tried to sit on one and landed on the floor.
That put him into a very bad mood.

Then they played Snakes and Ladders,
with *real* snakes and *real* ladders.
“I’ve never had so much fun!”
shouted Mouldylocks.
But the fun didn’t last.
Mama Kano cheated.

She climbed up the snakes instead of sliding down them.
"That's not fair!" cried Wizard Twittle.
He zapped a spell at Mama Kano but his sight
was poor and he zapped one of the snakes instead.
That's when the party began to get silly.

Mama Kano zapped Wizard Twittle.
"Take that, you twitty old grasshopper!"

But Wizard Twittle zapped her back.
"Take that, you slippery snail!"

Crabby Ann was crabbier than ever.
"Take that, you silly centipede!" she squawked,
firing a horrible spell at Mouldylocks.
But Mouldylocks was quick.
She hid behind a mirror. The spell hit the glass,
bounced off, and hit Crabby Ann fair and square.

"Now that was the silliest game of all," said Mouldylocks.
"Well, don't just stand there," croaked Mama Kano.
"Change us back again!" squeaked Crabby Ann.
"But I don't know any changing-back spells,"
said Mouldylocks.
"The book! The book!" chirped Wizard Twittle.
"Look in your birthday book of spells!"

"Here it is!" shouted Mouldylocks,
"on page 55, a spell for undoing spells."
She read out the recipe:

One pint of puddle water
One chopped mandrake root
Two salamander eggs
Half a spider's web
An owl's feather
One mug of cactus juice
Five drops of batspit

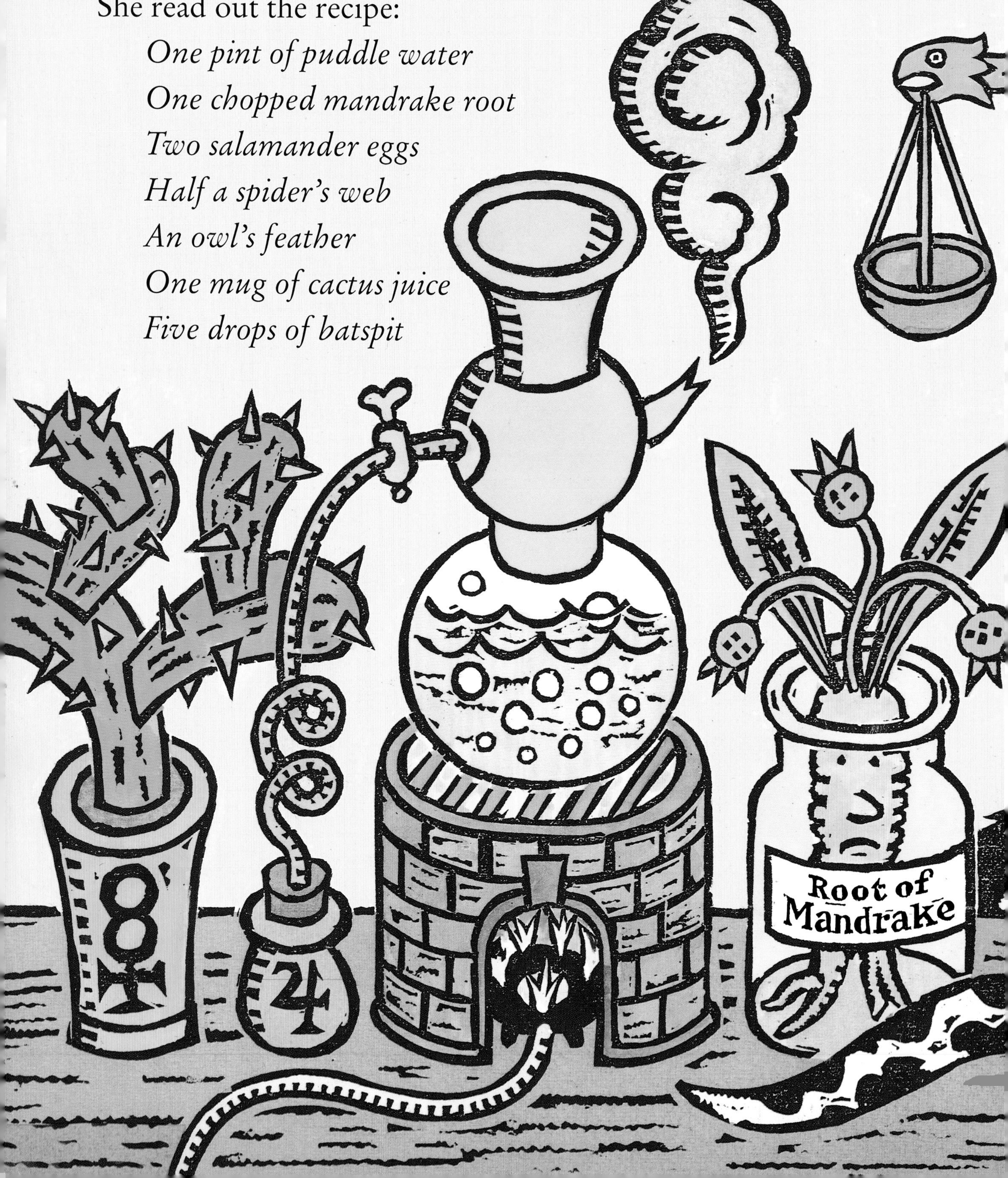

Well, the wizard's kitchen had just about everything that Mouldylocks needed, except cactus juice and batspit.

"Lots of cactus but no squeezer," said Mouldylocks.

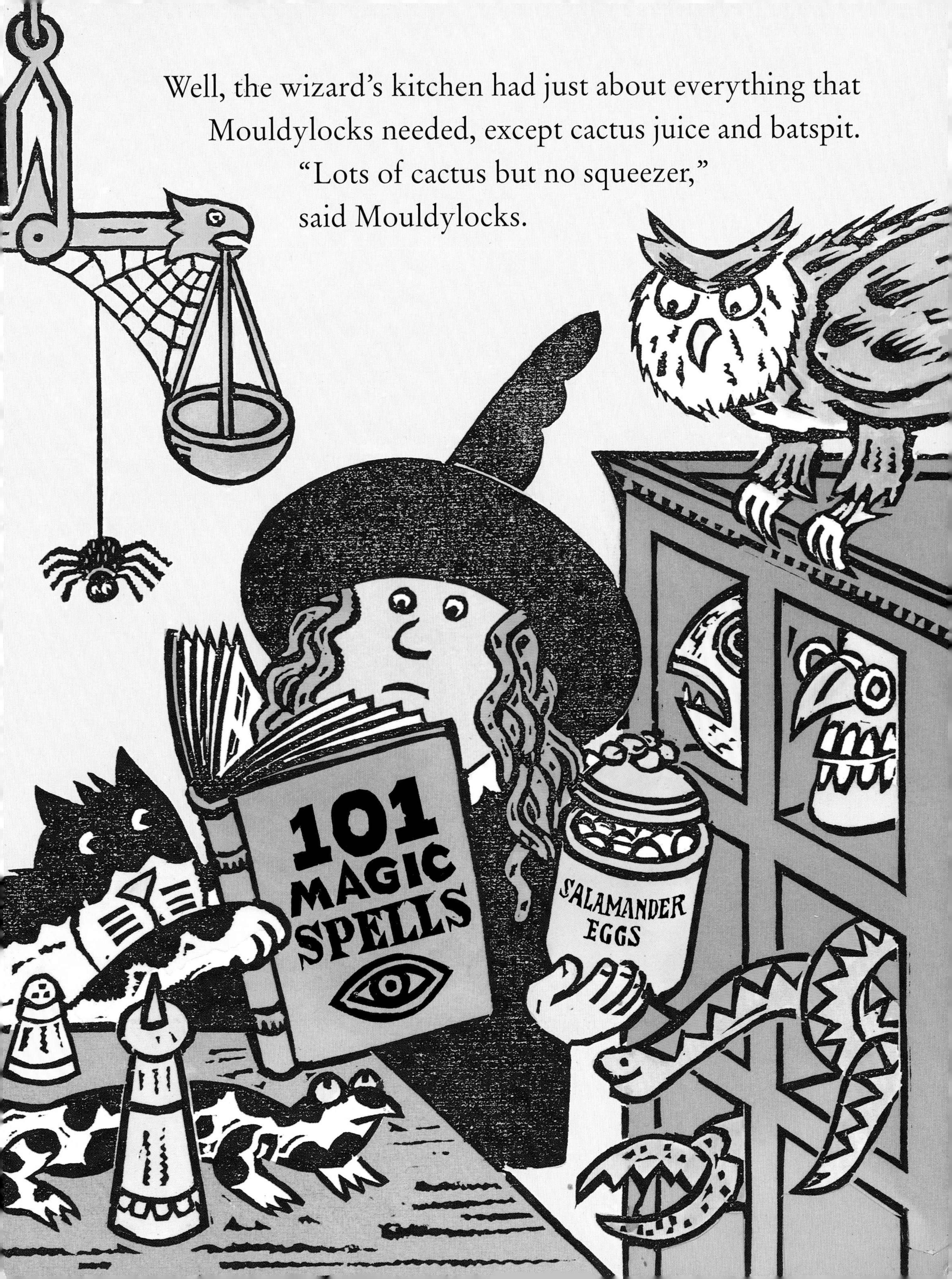

“Use your new boots,”
purred Hannibal.
“Those talking, walking boots
could mash a cactus in seconds.”
And they did.

"All I need now is batspit," said Mouldylocks.
"I've got my bat-in-a-box but how do I make it spit?"
"Easy!" said Hannibal, and he hissed at the bat
till it was spitting mad.
"That's enough, Hannibal!" cried Mouldylocks.
"We only need five drops."

Mouldylocks stirred the horrible brew
and poured it over her friends
as she said the magic words,
"HAZZAKA BAZZAKA HEXIT NEXIT!"
At once, the place filled with
smelly yellow smoke, and out of it staggered
Wizard Twittle, Crabby Ann and Mama Kano.

"Good old Mouldylocks," said Crabby Ann.
"How can we thank you?" said Mama Kano.
"What about a magic surprise?" said Wizard Twittle.
"No thanks," said Mouldylocks. "I've had enough surprises."
But she was too late. The wizard had spoken.

This was his surprise - a gigantic birthday cake.
It was so big that Mouldylocks
needed a snake and ladder
to reach the top.

"Now, blow out the candles," said Wizard Twittle.
"And make a wish," said Mama Kano.
"But hurry up," said Crabby Ann.
"I'm starving!"

Walter Lorraine (WL) Books

First Houghton Mifflin edition 1998
Originally published in Great Britain in 1998
Published by arrangement with Reed International Books Limited
Michelin House, 81 Fulham Road, London SW3 6RB

Library of Congress Cataloging-in-Publication Data
Lodge, Bernard.
Mouldylocks / Bernard Lodge.
p. cm.
Summary: When things get out of control at her surprise birthday
party, Mouldylocks, the witch, concocts just the right spell to restore order.
ISBN 0-395-90945-7
[1. Witches—Fiction. 2. Birthdays—Fiction. 3. Parties—Fiction.] I. Title.
PZ7.L8197Mo 1998
[E]—dc21 97-51183
CIP
AC

Printed in Dubai
10 9 8 7 6 5 4 3 2 1